The Three Little Pigs

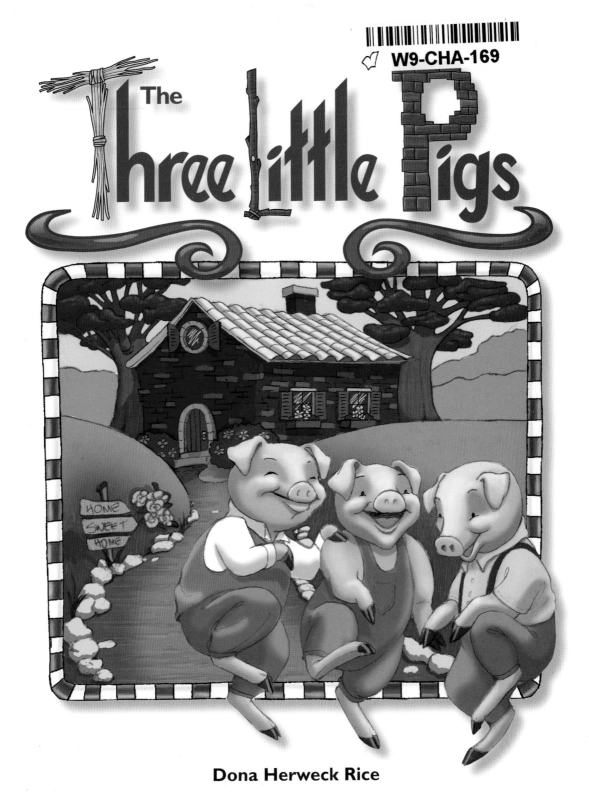

Dona Herweck Rice

Editorial Director
Dona Herweck Rice

Assistant Editors
Leslie Huber, M.A.
Katie Das

Editor-in-Chief
Sharon Coan, M.S.Ed.

Editorial Manager
Gisela Lee, M.A.

Creative Director
Lee Aucoin

Illustration Manager/Designer
Timothy J. Bradley

Illustrator
Karen Lowe

Publisher
Rachelle Cracchiolo, M.S.Ed.

Teacher Created Materials
5301 Oceanus Drive
Huntington Beach, CA 92649-1030
http://www.tcmpub.com
ISBN 978-1-4333-0170-4
© 2008 Teacher Created Materials, Inc.

The Three Little Pigs

Story Summary

This is a story about three little pigs. The pigs are ready to leave home. It is time for them to grow up and live on their own. So each pig builds a house to live in.

The first pig is lazy. That pig's house is made of straw. The straw bends and breaks. The second pig is silly. That pig's house is made of sticks. The sticks snap and crack. The third pig is smart. That pig's house is made of bricks. The bricks are strong. They will last a long time.

Trouble starts soon after the pigs build their houses. A big bad wolf moves nearby. The wolf likes to eat little pigs! Will the three little pigs be safe from the wolf? Will their houses last? Read the story to find out.

Tips for Performing Reader's Theater

Adapted from Aaron Shepard

- Don't let your script hide your face. If you can't see the audience, your script is too high.

- Look up often when you speak. Don't just look at your script.

- Talk slowly so the audience knows what you are saying.

- Talk loudly so everyone can hear you.

- Talk with feelings. If the character is sad, let your voice be sad. If the character is surprised, let your voice be surprised.

- Stand up straight. Keep your hands and feet still.

- Remember that even when you are not talking, you are still your character.

- Narrator, be sure to give the characters enough time for their lines.

Tips for Performing
Reader's Theater *(cont.)*

- If the audience laughs, wait for them to stop before you speak again.

- If someone in the audience talks, don't pay attention.

- If someone walks into the room, don't pay attention.

- If you make a mistake, pretend it was right.

- If you drop something, try to leave it where it is until the audience is looking somewhere else.

- If the reader forgets to read his or her part, see if you can read the part instead, make something up, or just skip over it. Don't whisper to the reader!

- If a reader falls down during the performance, pretend it didn't happen.

The Three Little Pigs

Characters

Narrator

First Pig

Second Pig

Third Pig

Wolf

Peddler

Setting

This reader's theater takes place in the country. There are three houses there. One house is made of straw. One house is made of sticks. One house is made of bricks.

Act 1

Narrator: A long road winds through the country. Three little pigs walk on that road. They have just left home. They are off to seek their fortunes in the world.

First Pig: At last! Now I can do what I want all day long. This is the life.

Second Pig: I will play all day.

Third Pig: Who will do the work?

First Pig: Mom will.

Second Pig: And Dad will, too.

Third Pig: You two are lazy and silly! Now we are grown up. We must take care of ourselves.

First Pig: But who will make my dinner?

Second Pig: How will I know what to do?

Third Pig: We can build our houses near one another. Then I can help you. And you can help me, too.

First Pig: Okay!

Second Pig: Good idea!

Narrator: The pigs walk on. Soon they meet a peddler. The peddler is selling straw.

Peddler: Would you like to buy this straw? You can make many things with it. You can make a hat. You can make a mat.

First Pig: Can you make a house?

Peddler: No. A straw house will bend and break.

First Pig: But it will be easy to build. Right?

Peddler: Yes. It will be very easy to build. You will just need straw and string.

First Pig: Sold!

Narrator: The first pig buys all the straw.

Second Pig: You are just lazy!

Third Pig: You will be sorry. Your house will not last.

Narrator: The first pig finds a shady spot under a tree. This is where the pig builds the house made of straw. The house is built in no time at all.

First Pig: Ah! That was fast. Now it is time to sleep.

Narrator: While the first pig sleeps, the other pigs walk down the road. Once again, they meet a peddler. Now the peddler is selling sticks.

Peddler: Would you like to buy these sticks? You can make many things with them. You can make a basket. You can make a nest.

Second Pig: Can you make a house?

Peddler: No. A stick house will snap and crack.

Second Pig: But it will be fun to build. Right?

Peddler: Yes. It will be very fun to build. It will be like building a toy house.

Second Pig: Sold!

Narrator: The second pig buys all the sticks.

Third Pig: You will be sorry. Your house will not last.

Narrator: The second pig finds a shady spot under a tree. This is where the pig builds the house made of sticks. The house is very fun to build.

Second Pig: Ah! That was fun. Now it is time for play!

Song: Skip to My Lou

Narrator: While the second pig plays, the third pig walks down the road. Once again, the pig meets a peddler. This time, the peddler is selling bricks.

Peddler: Would you like to buy these bricks? You can make many things with them. You can make a wall. You can make a chimney.

Third Pig:　Can you make a house?

Peddler:　Yes! A brick house will be strong.

Third Pig:　It will last a long time. Right?

Peddler:　Yes. It will last a very long time. You will be safe in a house made of bricks.

Third Pig:　Sold!

Narrator:　The third pig buys all the bricks. Then the pig finds a shady spot under a tree. This is where the pig builds the house made of bricks. The house is very strong.

Third Pig:　Ah! That was good work. Now it is time to move in.

Act 2

Narrator: The three little pigs are now in their own houses. They think they are safe. They do not know that trouble is near!

Wolf: Here comes trouble!

Narrator: A big bad wolf has moved nearby. And that wolf likes to eat little pigs!

Wolf: I knew this would be a good place to live. Pork for dinner! Yum!

Narrator: The wolf is not a nice neighbor.

Wolf: Hey! I can hear you.

Narrator: Then be nice!

Wolf: Nice won't get me dinner!

Narrator: The wolf sets out to find the pigs.

Wolf: Here I come, little pigs. Where are you?

Poem: This Little Piggy

Wolf: Oh, I see a straw house. I know one of those pigs lives there.

Narrator: The wolf walks to the door and calls out.

Wolf: Little pig! Little pig! Let me come in.

First Pig: Not by the hair of my chinny chin chin!

Wolf: Then I'll huff and I'll puff. And I'll blow your house in!

Narrator: The wolf huffs and puffs and blows the house in!

First Pig: Wee, wee, wee!

Narrator: The first pig runs to the stick house.

Wolf: Okay, fine. I will have two pigs for dinner.

Narrator: The wolf walks to the door of the stick house and calls out.

Wolf: Little pigs! Little pigs! Let me come in.

Narrator: The second pig sees the wolf from the window.

Second Pig: Not by the hair of my chinny chin chin!

Wolf: Then I'll huff and I'll puff. And I'll blow your house in!

Narrator: The wolf huffs and puffs and huffs and puffs. The wolf blows the house in.

First and Second Pig: Wee, wee, wee!

Narrator: Both pigs run to the brick house.

Act 3

Narrator: The third pig is safe in the brick house.

First and Second Pig: Wee, wee, wee!

First Pig: Let us in!

Second Pig: The wolf is coming!

Narrator: The third pig opens the door. In rush the other pigs.

First Pig: Quick, lock the door!

Second Pig: Oh, dear! What will we do?

Third Pig: I know. There is a fireplace in the house. Just wait to see what happens.

First Pig: I hope you know what you are doing!

Third Pig: Trust me.

Narrator: Just then, the wolf comes to the door.

Wolf: Little pigs! Little pigs! Let me come in.

Third Pig: Not by the hair of my chinny chin chin!

Wolf: Then I'll huff and I'll puff. And I'll blow your house in!

Narrator: The wolf huffs and puffs and huffs and puffs and huffs and puffs. But the wolf can not blow that house in!

Third Pig: Ha! You can not get in! The only way in is down the chimney. Ha! We will not be your dinner.

Wolf: Oh, yeah? Just wait and see.

Narrator: The wolf climbs up to the roof. Then the wolf jumps down the chimney!

Wolf: It is a little warm in here. Ouch! Ouch! It is very warm in here. Oh, no! Fire!

Narrator: The wolf climbs up the chimney as quick as can be. Then the wolf runs down the road.

Wolf: Wee, wee, wee!

Narrator: And that is the last the pigs see of the big bad wolf.

First and Second Pig: We weren't afraid!

Third Pig: Sure you weren't. Is that a huff and a puff I hear at the door?

First and Second Pig: Aaahhhhhh!

Third Pig: Who's afraid of the big bad wolf now?

This Little Piggy

Traditional

This little piggy went to market.
This little piggy stayed home.
This little piggy had roast beef.
This little piggy had none.
And this little piggy went "Wee, wee, wee!"
All the way home.

 # Skip to My Lou
Traditional

Fly's in the buttermilk, shoo, fly, shoo!
Fly's in the buttermilk, shoo, fly, shoo!
Fly's in the buttermilk, shoo, fly, shoo!
Skip to my Lou, my darlin'.

Chorus:
Skip, skip, skip to my Lou.
Skip, skip, skip to my Lou.
Skip, skip, skip to my Lou.
Skip to my Lou, my darlin'.

Cat's in the cream jar, ooh, ooh, ooh!
Cat's in the cream jar, ooh, ooh, ooh!
Cat's in the cream jar, ooh, ooh, ooh!
Skip to my Lou, my darlin'.

Chorus

Glossary

buttermilk—the milk that remains after the butter is separated from the cream

chimney—a pipe or tube that will not burn but lets smoke escape from a fire

fireplace—an area used to light a fire in a house for warmth or for cooking

fortunes—wealth

neighbor—a person who lives near another person

peddler—a person who travels and sells goods

pork—the meat from a pig